NEPHRO

THE ICE LOBSTER

With special thanks to Michael Ford

www.beastquest.co.uk

ORCHARD BOOKS
338 Euston Road, London NW1 3BH
Orchard Books Australia
Level 17/207 Kent St, Sydney, NSW 2000

A Paperback Original
First published in Great Britain in 2014

A CIP catalogue record for this book is available from
the British Library.

ISBN 978 1 40832 855 2

1 3 5 7 9 10 8 6 4 2

Printed and bound by CPI Group (UK) Ltd, Croydon, CR0 4YY

The paper and board used in this paperback are natural recyclable
products made from wood grown in sustainable forests. The
manufacturing processes conform to the environmental regulations of
the country of origin.

Orchard Books is a division of Hachette Children's Books,
an Hachette UK company

www.hachette.co.uk

NEPHRO
THE ICE LOBSTER

THE PRIDE OF BLACKHEART

BY ADAM BLADE

> OCEANS OF NEMOS: DELTA QUADRANT, NORTH EAST

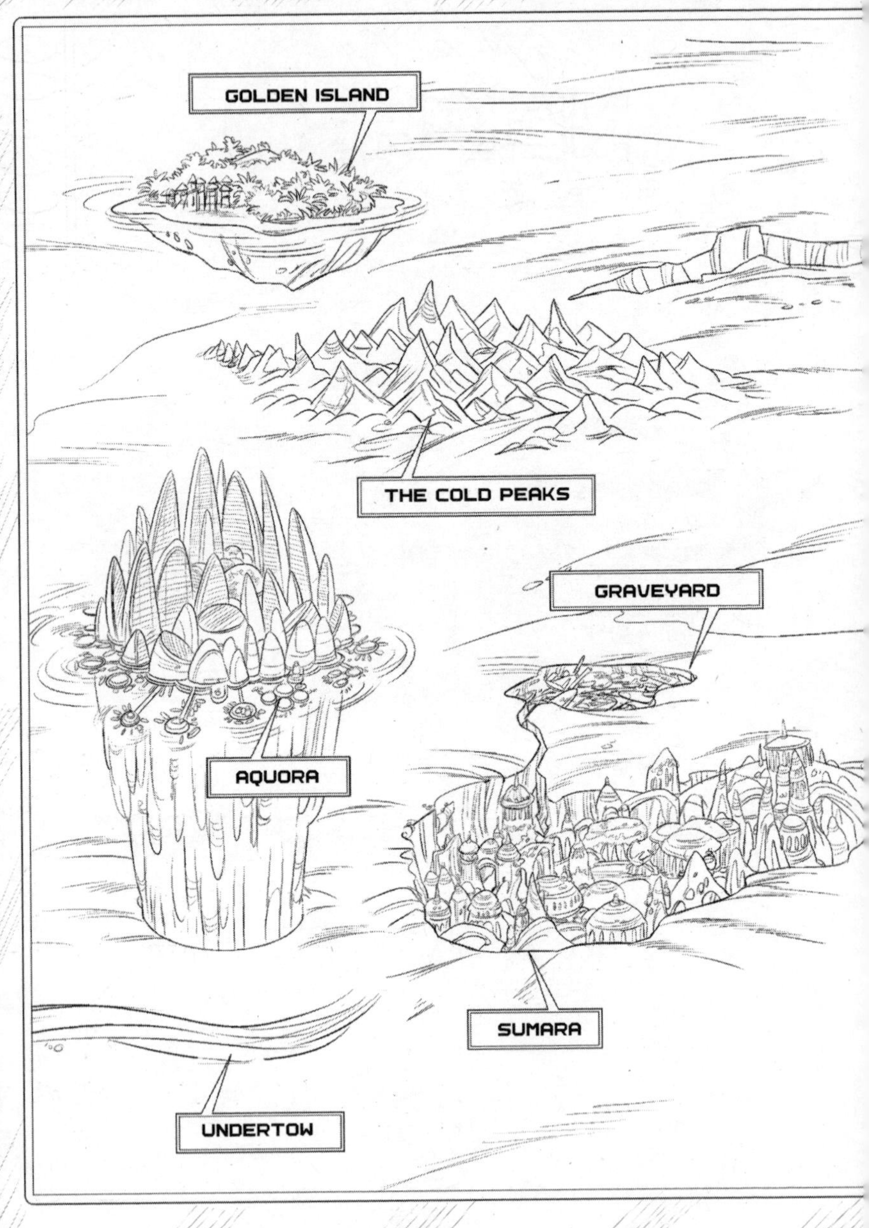

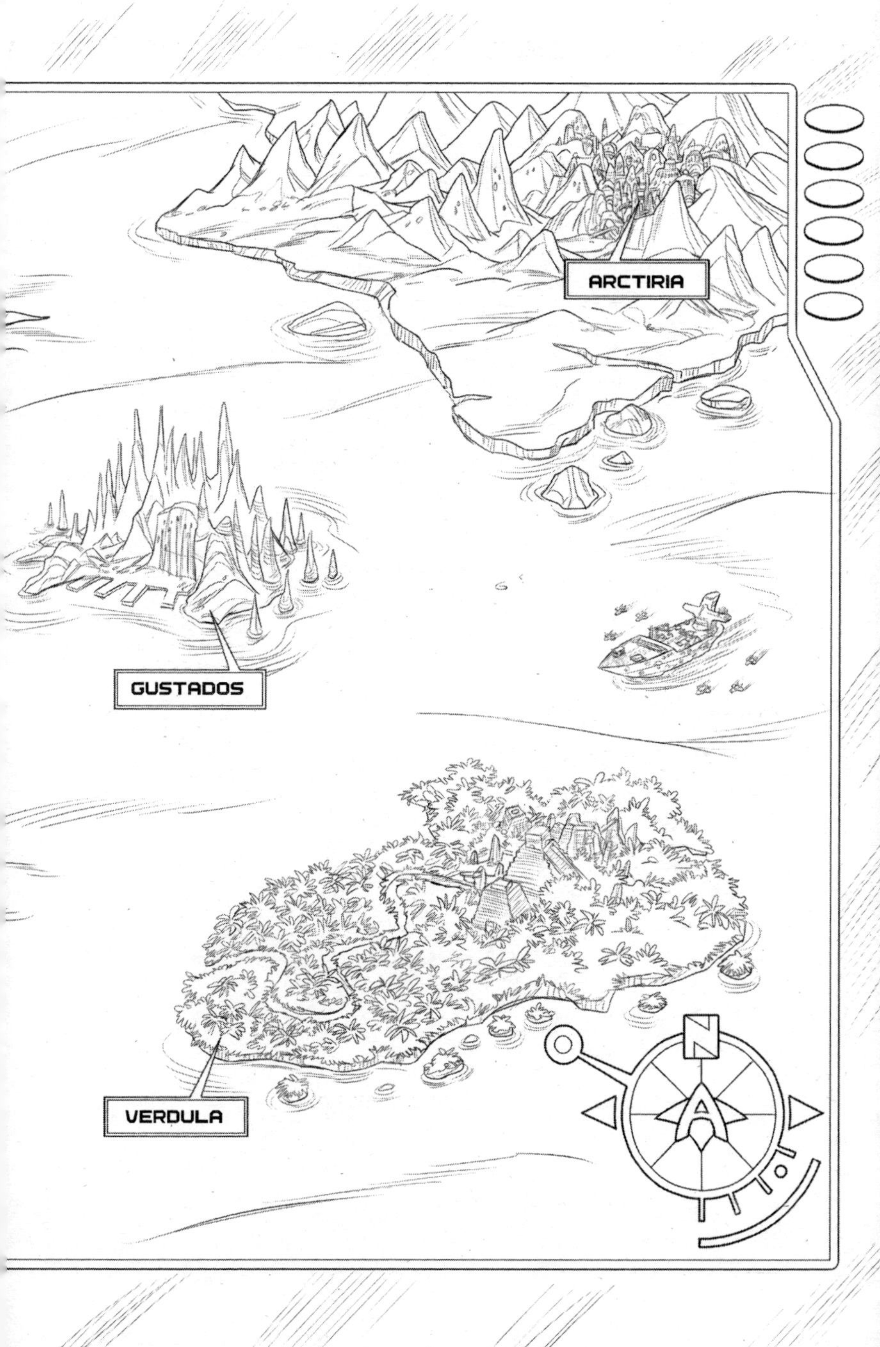
ARCTIRIA
GUSTADOS
VERDULA
N

>FROM: CAPTAIN REAVER OF THE *PRIDE OF DELTA*
>TO: THE DELTA QUADRANT ALLIANCE

URGENT – PLEASE RESPOND

Mayday! Hostile vessels were detected at 1632 hours off the starboard bow. The *Pride of Delta* has now been boarded by pirates. I am not sure how long we have…

Be aware, the Kraken’s Eye will soon be in the hands of the pirates. Please do whatever is necessary to secure the keys. The pirates must not be allowed to operate the weapon.

Rest assured I will not surrender the ship. We will remain in position until we receive a response, or until the ship is taken by force…

END

Message delivered: 1648 hours – Responses: 0

CHAPTER ONE

CHASING BLACKHEART

Max took one last look back at the jungle island of Verdula, enjoying the feel of the breeze against his cheeks. A figure appeared at the edge of the trees and waved a spindly hand before slipping out of sight.

"I hope the Verdulans will be left in peace for a long time," said Lia.

Max nodded and stared out to sea. The *Pride of Blackheart*, the stolen vessel crewed by Cora Blackheart's pirates, was just a distant dot on the horizon. Max and Lia had put a stop to her plans to raid the island by freeing Tetrax the Swamp Crocodile from his uncle the Professor's robotics.

Lia tore off her Amphibio mask and dived beneath the waves where she could breathe normally. Max was about to follow when he remembered the priceless object stored in his tunic pocket. He reached inside and took out the heavy iron key given to him by Naybor. Of all the treasures in the secret Verdulan city, this object was the most important. There were three other identical keys, and any one was enough to operate the Kraken's Eye, a deadly weapon that could destroy whole cities. Max dreaded to think what would happen if Cora controlled such a device.

Max slipped the precious key back inside his tunic pocket.

"Let's go, Riv," he said.

His aquabike kicked up foam as he gunned the engine and plunged beneath the water. Lia was waiting a few metres below the surface, sitting on Spike's back.

"What took you?" she asked.

Max glided the bike alongside her. "I was thinking," he said. "We should send a message to Aquora with the key. Let my dad know that we're chasing Cora and the pirates. He might be able to make plans or send backup."

Lia nodded. "I'll go," she said. "I know the seas better than you."

Max frowned. "That won't work. The *Pride of Blackheart* is cruising at full speed to Arctiria. It's in the opposite direction and..." He paused, searching for the words.

"And *what*?" said Lia.

"Well, I need you," Max said. "I can't tackle Cora Blackheart, the Professor *and* his

Robobeasts on my own."

Lia grinned. "Even with all your fancy technology?" she said, teasingly.

Max rolled his eyes.

Lia's smile grew wider. "Okay, so how do we send a message to your dad? I can't send an eel – your dad doesn't understand Merryn."

"Sometimes technology comes in useful," Max said, tapping the headset over his right ear. He hit the recall button and the dogbot paddled over. "Riv can take the message," he said, "and we can stay in touch via my headset." He touched Rivet's snout. "Riv, record," he said. Rivet's eyes flashed blue as the record function started.

"Dad," Max said. "No time to chat. A pirate called Cora Blackheart has stolen a Delta Quadrant Alliance ship, the *Pride of Delta*. She's working with the Professor to steal a key for the weapon on board, the Kraken's

Eye. We've got the Verdulan key – I'm putting it inside Rivet's secure compartment – but there are three more and she's heading to Arctiria next. Send help. Over and out."

"Does Rivet know the way to Aquora?" asked Lia.

"Thanks to technology, he does," said Max.

He twisted a small dial behind Rivet's ear, activating his "head for home" transmitter.

Rivet spun around, his nose pointing east. "Rivet warn Max's dad!" he barked. "Save Aquora!" His tail thrusters fired and he shot off through the water like a missile.

Max swallowed his sadness at watching the dogbot go. He switched on the aquabike's radar. The *Pride of Blackheart* was a flashing dot, heading north. "Come on, let's get after them," he said.

Spike flicked his tail and surged off. Max twisted the throttle in pursuit. Cora's ship was putting distance between them, but the aquabike's top speed was faster than the *Pride of Blackheart*.

Max stayed just behind Lia, following in her slipstream. He might have the best technology, but the Merryn girl could read the water better than any computer.

As they travelled north, the bike's temperature gauge plummeted. Max shivered. He noticed Lia had pulled her frilled suit tighter.

Max checked the radar. They were gaining ground on the *Pride of Blackheart*. "It won't be long now," he said, then couldn't resist adding, "Of course, I wouldn't know that if it weren't for *technology*."

Lia didn't have a smart answer for once. Max glanced sideways and couldn't see her anywhere.

"Slow down a bit," she called weakly.

Max turned and saw Spike had fallen behind. On his back, Lia's shoulders sagged. Her pale skin was almost blue, and her teeth were chattering madly. Even Spike looked tired, his eyelids drooping. Now Max thought about it, it was getting very cold indeed. He slowed down so the swordfish could keep up.

Perhaps there's a way I can pull them along.

Max fished in the storage compartment and found a bit of rope. Looping one end around the seat, he threw the other end to Lia. "Here, tie this on."

Lia's hands were trembling, but she managed to fasten the rope over Spike's fin.

"Th-th-thanks," she said.

Max was going to say something else about the benefits of technology, but Lia looked so sorry for herself, he thought better of it. He opened the aquabike's engines to full throttle and set off again.

But the extra weight slowed down the bike. Max checked the radar and saw Cora's vessel putting more distance between them. Soon they'd be off the scope completely.

"It's not working," said Lia. "We'll never catch Cora before she reaches Arctiria."

The thought of his uncle's smug face

flashed in Max's mind. The Professor knew he was no match for Max on his own. That was why he'd teamed up with Cora and built more Robobeasts.

I've not come this far to be defeated, Max thought.

"Here's an idea," he said, prising open the bike's control panel. "I can re-route some of the less important systems to the main power generator." He tinkered with the circuits. "We don't really need navigation systems or comms," he said, switching off a couple of circuit boards. He took a few other functions offline too, including the braking thrusters. "There! That should give us a bit more kick." He closed the panel. "Ready?"

Lia nodded, limbs quivering. "I hope you know what you're doing."

"Hang on," said Max. He opened the thrusters to full power and the bike jerked into motion. "Whoopee!" he yelled. He could barely keep his grip on the handlebars as the bike zipped along. Currents rammed into them like walls of water, tossing them around. He checked over his shoulder and saw Lia leaning close to Spike's back, panic written on her face.

With no navigation, Max relied on the

bike's compass to take them north, roughly in the direction of the pirate ship. He didn't have time to think about the cold any more – he just had to concentrate on not falling off!

"This is fun…right?" he called to Lia over the water's rush. "We should catch Cora in no time!"

Lia shouted something back, but he couldn't hear her.

"What's that?" he said, turning round.

The Merryn girl was pointing urgently ahead, her eyes wide. "I said – LOOK OUT!" she shouted.

Max spun round and saw an enormous hull of dark steel looming in the water ahead. The *Pride of Blackheart.*

He hit the brakes, but nothing happened. The bike raced full speed towards the ship.

Uh-oh!

CHAPTER TWO

INTRUDER ALERT

"Stop this thing!" Lia screamed.

Then Max remembered…

"I deactivated the brakes!" he yelled.

Twenty bike-lengths from the hull and certain death, Max killed the engine and yanked the handlebars upwards. The bike's nose lifted, but they were still on a collision course. Max heaved harder, until he thought his shoulders would pop from their sockets. The *Pride of Blackheart* filled his vision. He squeezed his eyes shut and braced for impact.

It never came.

Max opened one eye. They were drifting parallel to the barnacle-encrusted hull.

"Phew!" he gasped. "That was close."

He flicked a switch and the bike clamped onto the side of the enormous ship.

"How did it do that?" asked Lia.

Max grinned. "Magnets. Just another bit of tech I've been working on. Looks like it works, huh?"

Lia smiled wearily, then gestured with a nod of her head. "What's that?"

Max turned and saw a mounted camera and spotlight on the side of the ship. It swivelled, sweeping arcs of light underwater.

"Security!" said Max. "Looking for attackers below the waterline. We have to hide."

Lia slid off Spike and swam to a patch

of hull covered in mossy seaweed. She tore off a large section and dragged it back to the aquabike. "This will hide us!" she said proudly. She ripped a section for Max to drape over himself and laid the biggest piece over the bike. "Now we'll blend in."

"We just have to hope they don't have infrared or X-ray sensors," said Max.

Lia looked at him blankly.

"Never mind," he said.

The camera's light moved close to them. Max froze and held his breath, expecting to hear an alarm sound at any moment. To his relief, there was nothing.

"We can't stick around," he said. "Let's try and find a way onto the ship."

As the searchlight swept across the hull, Max quickly reactivated the circuit boards he'd disabled. Then he switched off the magnets and steered the aquabike slowly towards the front of the ship. He saw more cameras, but dodged their line of sight, sticking to the shadows.

As the bike crept almost silently beneath the ship, Max began to relax. *We might just survive this…*

He scanned the vast expanse of the hull. He'd studied ships like this at school back

in Aquora – there would be an underwater airlock somewhere. They just had to find it.

Lights approached through the water ahead. Max brought the bike to a halt.

"It's all right," said Lia. "They're just luminas, a type of jellyfish."

Max watched as the swarm of glowing bodies glided across the bottom of the ship.

They were almost see-through but for the pulsing lights at their centre, shining through their delicate frilly strands. Spike thrashed his sword, suddenly interested.

"We must be a long way north," said Lia, holding Spike's fin to keep him back. "Luminas only live in the very coldest waters. Spike's never seen them before."

The luminas changed direction all at once, as if following the moves of a dance.

"They're beautiful," said Max, leaning forward out of his seat.

"They're dangerous too," said Lia, pulling him back. "Deadly stingers. Just wait for them to pass."

But the luminas shifted again, moving directly towards them. "Oh no!" said Lia.

"I'll scare them off," said Max. He engaged the thrusters, sending out a blast of bubbles. The luminas rippled but kept coming.

Spike surged free of Lia's grip.

"No, Spike!" said Lia. "It's not a game!"

The swordfish dashed towards the luminas, emitting high-pitched squeaks. He passed straight through a swinging searchlight.

The luminas scattered as Spike plunged into the centre of the shoal, and at the same time the searchlight turned blood-red and began to flash.

"INTRUDERS! INTRUDERS! INTRUDERS!" barked an alarm.

Max grabbed Lia's arm. "Jump on!" he said.

With Lia on the bike, Max steered away from the light. Spike was still toying with the luminas, chasing them and getting nowhere near. "Get over here!" Lia yelled.

A section of the hull directly ahead began to slide back. A sleek one-man vessel, twice the size of the aquabike, nosed out. Max remembered them from his lessons – a Quadrant Intercept-Destroy sub, or 'QID' for short. *The latest in army tech!* And it wasn't just one. Max's stomach turned as at least a dozen QIDs slid out from the ship's underbelly. But where the Quadrant Alliance logo should have been on the sides, someone had scrawled skulls and crossbones.

Max twisted the bike away, but the QIDs moved quicker, taking up positions all around him. They closed in like a net. Suddenly the water seemed even colder.

"We're surrounded!" said Lia.

Max couldn't see Spike anywhere. He hoped the swordfish was hiding.

A final sub emerged from the ship, defaced with a different symbol – a jet-black heart.

"Cora Blackheart," said Max.

As the QID swung to face him, he saw his enemy through the plexiglass bubble of the cockpit. The pirate leader glared at him, her neck laden with gold chains. Gold hoops dangled from her ears.

She raised a finger adorned with golden rings, the nail long like a talon.

Then she grinned and drew the finger in a slow line across her throat.

CHAPTER THREE

DOGFIGHT

"What have we here?" said Cora, through the sub's microphone. "Stowaways, I think."

Max's heart was thumping, but he did his best not to look scared. "We're going to stop you, Cora, just like we did on Verdula."

Cora's eyes narrowed. "Give me the key and I'll let you live," she said.

Max fought the temptation to look down towards his inside pocket. "Too late," he said. "I've already sent my dogbot back to Aquora with it. You'll never operate the Kraken's Eye."

Cora smiled cruelly. "Well, then," she said, "there's no reason not to kill you right now."

Her fingers moved over the control panel and a launch tube dropped from the QID's base. Max engaged the downward thrusters as a torpedo sped towards them. The shot scorched through the water and slammed into another QID at their rear. It exploded into fragments. The pirate inside started clawing desperately towards the surface.

"Nice try," said Max.

"Little maggots," screeched Cora. "Pirates, attack positions and cannons loaded, all of you!"

Cannons bristled from every sub and the water suddenly lit up with blasters.

"Time to go!" said Max. "Hold on tight!" He sent the aquabike through the gap where the vaporised sub had been. From the corner of his eye, he thought he saw Spike darting along below, just a shadow in the gloomy water.

"After those weevils!" Cora yelled.

Max jerked the handlebars from side to side to make the bike a harder target to hit.

More shots passed perilously close.

"They're gaining!" yelled Lia beside him.

Of course they are, thought Max. QIDs were the fastest attack vessels the Quadrant's navy had. He felt like a goldfish fleeing a school of sharks.

Max put the bike into a steep dive. He couldn't outrun the QIDs, but he might be able to outmanoeuvre them. To his dismay, he saw the subs fanning out. Cora's pirates weren't stupid. They'd simply surround him again, and close in.

Despite the blood pumping through his veins, the cold water hugged him like a coat of ice. Their pursuers were protected from the freezing sea, but Max could feel his reactions slowing.

"I can't keep this up for long," he said as a torpedo zipped past them, trailing bubbles. "We need a plan."

"I know!" said Lia. "The Pearls of Honour."

Max felt her shift behind him, reaching for the magical Pearls pinned to her tunic.

He hoped they brought help quickly. Preferably something big.

An angry whale would be good!

A QID shot past, then turned to face them, its torpedo locked on the bike. Max looked left and right and saw more subs blocking any escape route. *We're finished*, he thought.

The torpedo fired, straight towards the bike. At the last moment a grey shape zipped out of nowhere, and knocked the missile off-target.

"Spike!" shouted Lia.

The brave swordfish swam towards them, and Lia leaped off the aquabike and onto his back.

"Let's s-split up!" she said, her teeth chattering. "G-give them two moving targets.

They won't be able to catch us both."

A blaster bolt sizzled right between them.

"Good luck," said Max.

He banked away, and five QIDs came with him, including Cora's. He sensed a sub coming from his right, and dipped just in time as a torpedo trailed overhead. Two more QIDs came from dead ahead in a pincer movement.

Then Max saw it. A huge shape moving from the depths.

Not a whale…

Max gasped. It was some sort of giant walrus, as big as a transport sub. Two tusks, as long as Max was tall, jutted out beneath a bushy moustache. Rolls of blubbery fat shook as the creature butted right into one of the QIDs, knocking it aside and cracking its hull like an eggshell.

Max cheered. "Over there!" he said,

pointing to the remaining subs. "Chomp them all up."

The QIDs backed away as one, and Max realised Cora must have given an order to retreat. But the creature didn't pursue them. Instead it rolled lazily in the water.

Max frowned, confused. "Attack!" he shouted.

The walrus turned slowly to Max, twitched its moustache, and burped.

This isn't working, thought Max. *It doesn't understand.*

Below him, he saw Lia, holding the glowing Pearls aloft. "Help us," she pleaded.

The walrus dipped his stubby nose and swam towards her. *That's better*, thought Max. *At least it's listening.*

The creature floated right up to Lia, opened its mouth, and snatched the Pearls from her.

"No!" said Lia. "You can't!"

Tossing back its head, the walrus swallowed the Pearls in a single mouthful. Stunned, Max watched it slowly swim away. He steered the bike towards Lia.

"This can't be happening," he said. "So much for helping us!"

Lia sighed. "I suppose the Pearls just attract

the creatures," she said. "Unfortunately they don't all have the heroic instinct. Some are just hungry."

Cora's subs began to press closer.

"Well, the only instinct I've got at the moment is survival," Max said, shaking off his frustration. "Let's go!"

Side by side, they shot away from the *Pride of Blackheart* and their enemies. The subs gave chase, all guns blazing. Max's radar registered nine blobs speeding in their wake, incredibly fast. Blaster bolts and torpedoes shot past, missing them by metres. But they'd find their range soon, Max knew. They needed somewhere to hide. He risked a glance back over his shoulder and saw Cora's sub edging ahead of the others. Her face wore a cruel grin.

That shark smells blood, he thought.

Then another object appeared on the

screen. Something huge, filling the screen slightly to the north-west. *Another ship, maybe?*

"Follow me!" shouted Max, changing course.

Soon he saw it. Not a ship, but a wall, descending far into the depths. It shone pale blue through the dark sea.

"Ice!" said Lia.

Max's heart sank. *Not another obstacle.* "Can you see a way through?" he asked desperately.

Lia pointed. "There! A crack!"

Max saw it too, a narrow fissure in the solid wall. Just wide enough for the aquabike.

Probably.

The bike shook as the engines worked at capacity. The lasers were coming closer. It wouldn't be long.

Almost there…

Spike gave an extra kick and shot through the gap, carrying Lia. Max tipped the bike sideways to fit. Its left thruster caught the lip of the crack and broke off with a screech of shearing metal. Max tumbled off the aquabike as it turned over, rolling across the ice. With thumping scrapes, the bike slid to a halt on the ground.

Lia appeared beside Max and helped him to his feet. They were in some sort of ice cave, he realised. "Are you all right?" Lia asked.

"Just a few bruises," he said. "You?"

"Glad to be alive," she said.

The ground shook and the air lit up as laser blasts struck the wall outside. But the ice was thicker than Aquora's defensive walls. It would take something nuclear even to make a dent.

"We're safe," he said, breathing a sigh of relief. "For a while, at least."

Lia started to shiver violently. "Safe, but freezing," she said. "We can't stay in here for long."

The shots from outside had stopped. "Perhaps they've given up," said Max.

He went to the edge of the crack and peered through. *Zumf!* A blaster crunched into the ice, almost scorching his nose off. Max ducked back inside.

"Or p-p-perhaps not," said Lia. Her lips were trembling.

Max tried to warm her by rubbing her arms. Soon cold stole over his limbs, and his teeth were chattering as well. *Cora knows we can't hold out in here*, he realised. *She's just waiting for us to freeze to death.*

"We could surrender," he said, looking uncertainly at Lia. "I escaped the *Pride of Blackheart* once before…"

"With m-m-my help," said Lia, crouching

to the floor in a ball. "We c-can't risk the K-Kraken's Eye falling into…"

Lia's eyes glazed over as her words trailed off. She fell slowly to one side, and Max caught her in his arms.

"Lia?" he said, his heart somersaulting. "Lia!"

His friend said nothing.

CHAPTER FOUR

PRISON OF ICE

"Wake up!" Max said, giving Lia a shake. "We haven't come this far to die in a cave!"

Lia's eyelids fluttered briefly, but her eyes remained closed.

Max felt his frustration boiling over. "Stupid ice!" he shouted, punching the wall.

Pain shot through his arm, but Max ignored it. His ears had picked up a strange hollow sound. He gave the ice a kick and heard it again. Almost like there was something on the other side. *Another cave?*

He let Lia float in the water, and ran his finger over the ice. "Maybe it leads to the surface..." he muttered, hope rising in his chest.

Spike swam to his side, nodding his sword up and down at the wall.

When Max had first met Spike, the swordfish had used his bill to break open the ZX200 Sea Lion craft Max was trapped in.

"Go on then!" said Max. "Get us out of here!"

Spike attacked the wall, slashing and sawing and stabbing. Ice particles flew everywhere. But Max could see at once that he was hardly making a dent, and his sword was flexing dangerously. He put a hand on the swordfish's flank. "That's enough, Spike. You did your best."

Spike tried half-heartedly to surge forward

again, but Max tugged him back. "Don't," he said. "You might break your sword completely."

"Come here, Spike," said Lia weakly. "Let me help."

Spike drifted alongside the Merryn girl, making odd wailing sounds. Lia reached out a trembling hand, and laid it on his sword. Her eyes closed and she drew a deep breath, her brow creasing in pain. As she breathed out again, Spike's sword began to glow deep orange like an ember.

Whoa! thought Max. *It must be her Merryn Aqua Powers again!*

Lia's arm fell limp once more, drained of energy.

Spike left her and swam back to the wall. Max could feel the heat coming from the sword, like a poker left in the fire. "That's amazing!" he muttered.

Spike slid the sword into the ice like a hot knife through butter. In no time at all, he'd created an opening. Water began to rush past Max through the hole. He felt himself being sucked towards it.

"There must be air on the other side," he muttered. Max swam to the bottom of the cave and heaved Lia upright. "We're getting out of here," he said, snatching the Amphibio mask from his friend's belt and looping it over her face and gills.

He dragged her towards the hole and bundled her through. Now they were in a larger ice cavern. The air was warmer, but water poured through the gap like a torrent. Max realised it wouldn't be long until the freezing seawater filled it completely. They had to find a way out. He glanced around desperately. Was that...?

Yes! A tunnel!

At the back of the cavern he spied an opening, leading into darkness.

It's our only chance.

"Lia," he said. "You're going to have to walk. I can't carry you over the ice."

A little colour had seeped back into her

cheeks, and she nodded weakly as she breathed through the mask. Max helped her stand. "What about Spike?" she said.

Max realised the swordfish was still watching them from the other side of the hole. His sword had lost its warm glow.

"We can't take him with us," Max said softly, "but we'll come back for him. I promise."

Lia reached through the gap and laid her webbed fingers over Spike's head. She didn't say anything, but Max knew she didn't need to. Spike nodded his sword and backed away.

"Let's go," said Lia.

Max led the way through ankle-deep water to the tunnel's entrance. The ice-covered walls looked black and blue in the semi-darkness. Who knew what they'd find in there?

The ground was slippery beneath his feet as he pressed on, running his hands along the ice wall. He heard Lia trip behind him and stopped. "Are you all right?"

His voice echoed through the tunnel.

"Yes," she said, straightening up. "Just getting my strength back. Where do you think this goes?"

Max shrugged, walking on. The tunnel sloped gently upwards. "Who knows? But we can't go back now."

The ice walls all around shone deep blue, almost as if there was light on the other side. The slope became steeper, and Max found it harder than ever to stay on his feet. Soon he had to use his hands as well, half crawling, half walking. His fingers felt like frozen claws. He could hear Lia breathing hard.

They reached a section of the tunnel that was even steeper. Max tried to crawl up it, but slid back helplessly, scuffing his knees. He made another attempt, but just slipped down the shiny surface again.

"Let me go first," said Lia. She took a run-up, throwing herself at the slope and reaching with her hands. No luck. She fell back at Max's side.

"It's hopeless!" Lia said. "We'll never get up

there without some sort of help."

"Then we're trapped," said Max.

"At least nothing's trying to kill us," said Lia, managing a thin smile.

Her words were still echoing through the tunnel when another sound followed, deep and rumbling.

"What was that?" whispered Lia. A shiver ran down Max's spine.

"I think it was a growl," he said.

CHAPTER FIVE

POLAR MENACE

A shadow appeared at the top of the slope. A big shadow, its flanks rising and falling with steady breaths. The creature lifted its massive head and sniffed the air.

Max and Lia backed away down the tunnel, sliding on the ice.

The shape began to descend into the meagre light on all fours. Max saw pale fur, then a wedge-shaped head with small pricked-up ears. Yellow teeth were bared over black lips. "It's some sort of bear," he whispered. The creature's claws were as long as fingers, curling and razor-sharp, digging into the slope.

"I'll try and talk to it," said Lia. "If it lives beside the sea, maybe my Aqua Powers will work on it."

She stepped in front of Max and gave a series of whines. The bear lifted its head and stared at her with cold eyes. Then it rose up on its hind legs, opened its jaws and roared. Max realised his entire body would fit easily into that gaping mouth.

"It's not working," said Lia. "Maybe my Aqua Powers are drained. Or maybe it's just a land bear."

Max tugged her back, and stepped in front.

"What are you doing?" she said. "Are you mad?"

Probably, he thought, but he said, "I think I've got an idea."

Taking care not to look directly at the bear,

he gave a few soft clicks with his tongue. He'd trained Rivet to respond to ordinary dog-obedience commands. Perhaps the same would work for this monster. The key was not to engage in eye contact, in case they found it threatening. You had to earn their trust.

If this doesn't work, I'll be torn to pieces…

From the corner of his eye he saw the bear drop to all fours again, its lip curling in a slight snarl. Max's heart thumped so hard he was sure the bear could hear it. *Don't show fear*, he told himself. *Keep calm.* He continued to give reassuring clicks as he slowly held out his hand. It took all his courage not to let it shake.

The bear padded forward, then sniffed his fingers. It growled again, but more softly. Max dared to lift his gaze to meet the bear's. "It's all right," he whispered. "We're friends."

For the next few minutes he let the bear lead the way, sniffing and shuffling around

him. Lia stepped closer too and the creature investigated her as well. The bear arched its neck towards Max's face, until its teeth were a fraction from his cheek and he could feel the warmth of its breath.

Then it gave him a rough lick.

"I think it likes you," said Lia.

Max managed to smile. He stroked the bear's thick fur and it didn't seem to mind.

"I've got an idea how we can get up the slope," he said. Before he could talk himself out of it, Max gripped a handful of fur, braced one foot against the tunnel wall and clambered up onto the bear's back. The creature shifted slightly beneath him.

"You're kidding," said Lia.

"Jump on," said Max, patting the bear's side, and holding out a hand.

Lia shook her head as he helped her up. "You Breathers!" she said. "I'll never understand you."

"It's no different to you talking to underwater creatures," said Max. "Just think of the bear as a furry fish, if it makes you feel better."

As soon as they were both settled on its back, the bear turned around and began to climb the slope. The massive bulk shifted and swayed beneath them. The bear's claws dug into the ice with a solid grip and it carried them easily up the steep incline. Max hung on for dear life and Lia's hands clutched his waist.

Lia began to talk again, making strange whines and clicks. The bear grunted back.

"Your Aqua Powers are back?" said Max.

"Yes," said Lia. The colour had come back to her cheeks and her eyes sparkled with life. "Guess what! She says this is Arctiria."

"We made it!" said Max.

"She says the whole island is made of ice," said Lia. "Everyone lives in a huge iceberg – a mountain of icy tunnels and giant cavities."

"Are the Arctirians friendly?" asked Max.

Lia communicated with the bear again as they climbed.

"She says they can be a bit vain."

"What does she mean by that?" asked Max.

The tunnel widened ahead. Max hadn't noticed before, but now he realised the light was much more intense. The walls shone sky blue, as though the ice had thinned around them. As they reached the mouth of the tunnel and walked into open air, great crests and pillars of ice rose all around them under a perfect blue sky.

It's beautiful, Max thought.

"She says the Arctirians are strict about their personal space," said Lia. "We mustn't reach out or touch them. And under no circumstances wear anything red. They hate the colour because it symbolises fire, and they think it will threaten their ice-made home."

"Makes sense," said Max, with a shiver, "but..." He stopped as he heard something.

"Help!" came a cry. "Get away from me!"

Max nudged the bear's flanks and it took off at a run, bounding rapidly over the ice. Max's bones shook as he buried his hands in the bear's fur, trying to hold on.

"Help me!" screamed the voice. *A woman*, Max realised.

They reached the crest of a tall ledge of ice and the bear skidded to a halt. Max gasped. Looming in the distance was a mountain of ice, perfectly symmetrical and towering at least forty storeys tall. But just ahead he saw the strangest creatures he'd ever laid eyes on. They were nearly twice as tall as an adult human, with blue skin and willowy limbs. Their heads were long and narrow, with wide-spaced yellow eyes and strong features. They stood in a circle, and each was pointing and shouting angrily at a human woman in the middle. She had her back to Max and Lia.

"Hey!" said Max. "Leave her alone!"

The Arctirians spun around as one, looking terrified, and the woman standing in their midst turned more slowly.

Max's stomach seemed to drop away and his

skin froze in an instant.

It can't be.

He couldn't breathe. His limbs tensed and he felt rooted to the spot.

It can't be her.

"What's the matter?" asked Lia.

Max's tongue felt thick and unwieldy in his mouth. At last, he managed a single word.

"Mother?"

CHAPTER SIX

UNWELCOME VISITORS

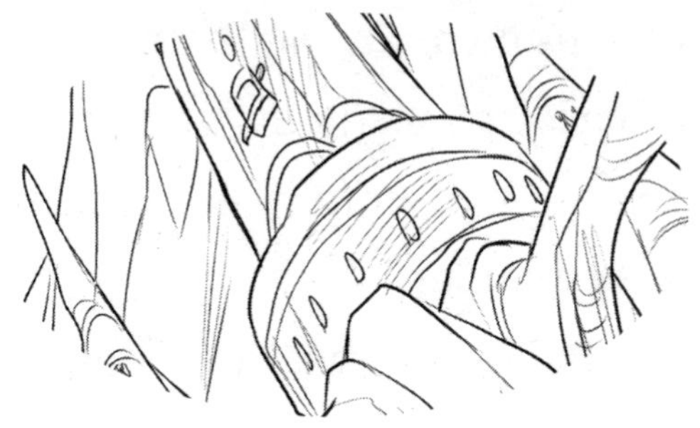

"Your mother?" whispered Lia. "Are you sure?"

Max slid down from the polar bear's back. *Am I sure? It's been so long.*

His legs felt wobbly, but he forced himself to move. He broke into a run. "Let her go!" he shouted.

One of the Arctirians blocked his path, seizing Max in a powerful grip. He strained to break free, but couldn't. His eyes were fixed on the woman. Her red hair fell to her shoulders. Her cheeks were more angular than he remembered, her lips thinner. Unsmiling. But it was her. He knew the face as well as his own.

"Mother?" he called out. "Is it you?"

"Max," she said simply. Her voice was flat, almost emotionless.

One of the Arctirians – a woman – turned to Max. He saw that close up these people were beautiful, with perfectly balanced features and skin that seemed to glow.

"Small one," she said. "This creature has offended us with her fiery robes. She tried to seize my hand as if I were some sort of pet."

Max noticed his mum's wetsuit had bold red panels. *She must have tried to shake hands with the Arctirian!* he thought.

"She meant no harm," said Lia, arriving at Max's side. "Where humans come from, taking another's hand is a sign of friendship."

A scowl of disgust crossed the Arctirian's face.

"Very well," she said. "Guards! Take these *humans* and this Merryn girl to the city. I can't stand looking at such ugly creatures any longer."

"Hey!" said Lia. "Who are you calling ugly?"

"You," said the Arctirian. "Now, begone!"

The guard holding Max grabbed Lia too. Another took hold of Max's mother. They were jostled towards the mountain of ice in the distance.

"Wait!" said Max. "We've come to warn you! Invaders are on the way."

"Invaders?" said the Arctirian leader. "We fear no one."

"Listen to him," said Lia desperately. "They're pirates. They're coming to steal the

key to the Kraken's Eye."

Max thought he saw a faint frown crossing the woman's blue face, but it was gone in a heartbeat. "What are you waiting for?" she said to the others. "Take them away."

The guards led Max, his mother and Lia across the ice, along a wide path. Soon they reached the mountain. They passed beneath an arch of sculpted ice and entered the

interior. Max craned his neck, marvelling at the strange architecture. Bridges spanned the heights above, and staircases linked the many levels. Here and there he saw openings into grand chambers and tunnels and domes of ice. Lia was goggling too, Max noticed. Only his mother stared straight ahead, seemingly unimpressed.

The whole space at the base of the ice

mountain was occupied by a great square, teeming with Arctirians, all impossibly beautiful. The blue inhabitants they passed all kept their distance, turning up their noses as if the visitors smelled bad.

"Not very friendly, are they?" whispered Lia.

The guards took them up flights of icy steps, higher into the mountain city. The Arctirians hardly seemed to be breathing at all, but Max's legs ached with the climb and he was panting hard.

His mother walked ahead with her back to him, not once turning to look around. *Why isn't she saying anything?* he wondered. *Perhaps she's waiting until we're alone.* He wanted to speak, but he hardly knew what to say. He hadn't seen her in the flesh since he was a toddler.

Several storeys up they reached a door.

"Wait in here," said one of the guards. He directed Max and the others into a chamber surrounded by spiky columns of ice. There were benches of ice too, but otherwise the room was empty. In places the ice wall was so thin it was transparent. Through these windows, Max could see the sky and sea beyond.

"Exactly how long are you planning to keep us here?" asked Lia. "Cora's pirates are coming!"

"We will investigate your claims, ugly one," said the guard. He left them, leaving two more tall Arctirians at the door.

"Charming!" said Lia.

Max turned to his mother. "Mum!" he cried, stepping closer to her. He opened his arms.

His mother merely nodded her head towards him. "Son," she said.

Max was puzzled. *She must be in shock too.* "Mum, where have you *been*?" he said.

His mother shrugged. "I went off on a research mission, on board the *Leaping Dolphin*. Maybe you don't remember. You were only young."

"That was ten years ago!" said Max.

"I've been busy," she said. "Very busy."

"Too busy to send a message?" said Max, his temper flaring. "Too busy to let us know you were alive?"

His mother turned away. "Don't be selfish, son," she said. "My work was important."

Max felt heartbroken. He glanced at Lia. She was watching him, her eyes full of sympathy. This didn't feel right at all. He'd dreamed of finding his mum one day, but this was nothing like his dreams.

She hasn't even tried to touch me…

A knock at the door made them all turn. An elderly man – a *human* man – was pushed into the room. His head was bald and he had a bushy white beard.

"Who are you?" asked Max's mum harshly.

"I'm Jonah," said the man. He walked with a stoop. "They sent me to talk with you, because it was I who made the keys to the Kraken's Eye."

"You?" said Max. "Cora Blackheart is coming for the key now. She's got a huge ship with enough tech to melt Arctiria to sea water."

The old man's wispy eyebrows rose a notch. "Cora, eh?"

"You know her?" asked Lia.

"I sailed with Cora many years ago," he said. "I was a different person then. On the ship of One-Eyed Roger."

Max almost fell over with surprise. "You mean Roger the pirate?" he said. "We've met him!"

"Not seen him for many a year," said Jonah. "Cora was his first mate, but she mutinied, and stole his ship. Left Roger marooned on a desert island, the wicked wretch. After that, I decided my pirate days were over. Came here to find a quiet life. I made the keys for that weapon. It was supposed to keep the seas in peace."

Max glanced out of the window. A dark shape loomed on the horizon. *The Pride of Blackheart*. "Well, they won't be peaceful for much longer," he said, pointing to the ship. "Cora wants the key to the Kraken's Eye and she'll kill to get it. I have to persuade the Arctirians to give it to me."

Jonah nodded slowly, and reached into his pale robes. He drew out the key.

"Consider them persuaded," he said.

CHAPTER SEVEN

ARCTIRIA UNDER ATTACK

Jonah pressed the key into Max's hand. "The Arctirians won't fight," he said. "They're pacifists. Take this key far away."

Max examined the iron key. Its shape was the same as the Verdulan version, but the symbols etched into the surface were stars and comets, rather like an ancient sea chart. He felt his mother's gaze on it too.

"Don't worry," he said. "We'll destroy all the keys. Then we'll deal with Cora."

Jonah's eyes hardened suddenly, and he gripped Max's shoulder with strong fingers. "You be careful, boy," he said. "Cora's not to be trifled with. She left Roger to the crabs on barely more than a sun-baked rock. Some say he went mad before he got away."

I can vouch for that, thought Max.

"We'll be careful," he said.

Jonah released his shoulder and gave the smallest of nods. "The guards will let you go now," he said. "Good luck." With those words, he shambled out of the chamber.

Max tucked the key inside his tunic. "That was easier than I expected," he said.

The guards at the door parted to let them pass. "We just need to find Spike," said Lia.

"And my aquabike," Max said. He turned to see his mother very close behind him. "You'll come with us, won't you?"

"Come with you?" she said, her face emotionless.

"Once we've found all the keys, we can go back to Aquora. Dad misses you so much. He thought you were… I mean…we had no news. You understand?"

"I understand," said his mother.

I mentioned Dad, and she didn't even flinch, thought Max. *She can't have forgotten him, surely!*

Suddenly, the ground beneath Max's feet rumbled and shook. A series of deafening cracks echoed through the ice mountain. Screams and shouts rose from all around.

"What is that?" asked Lia. "Cora's ship can't be here yet."

A waif-like Arctirian came running up a set of stairs. "It's terrible," he said. "We're being attacked!"

Another emerged from a passageway. "A monster in the tunnels!" he cried.

The female leader strode up to Max and his friends. "This is your fault!" she said. "I knew we should never have welcomed you here."

I'd hardly call it a welcome, thought Max. But he kept that to himself. "Gather your

forces," he said. "They mustn't get the keys."

"Forces?" said the Arctirian. "We don't have an army! Arctirians believe in peaceful solutions."

Blue people began streaming from several doors, all rushing downwards, pushing past Max and his friends. They were heading deeper into the ice mountain.

"Cora doesn't know the meaning of peaceful solutions," said Lia. "We need to fight her."

"We can't fight," said the Arctirian. "We're much too beautiful to put ourselves in danger. We'll hide until all this is over."

She joined the others rushing away. Max shot a desperate glance at his mother. "Will you fight with us?"

"I will," she said, "but they took my weapon to something they called their 'contraband cavern.'"

Sounds promising, Max thought. *Maybe there'll be other weapons there.*

He moved quickly and blocked one of the rushing Arctirians. "Where's the contraband cavern?" he asked.

The tall blue figure shied away from him. "Don't touch me, you hideous thing!" she said in disgust.

"Just tell us where it is, then!" said Lia.

Another quake shook the mountain from below and the Arctirian trembled. "It's two floors below," she said. "Follow the eastern passage and the contraband chamber is at the very end."

Max let her pass, and ran down the staircase, taking three steps at a time.

Two levels down, Max found the corridor deserted. With Lia and his mother close behind, he dashed along its length. The sound of smashing ice was growing closer.

It's a Robobeast, for sure, thought Max. What horror had the Professor come up with this time?

They reached a semi-transparent doorway of ice.

"How do we get through?" asked Lia.

Max couldn't see any sort of handle or

lock on the door. "The old-fashioned way," he said. Taking a step back, he launched his foot at the door. Pain jarred his ankle as a spider's-web crack appeared. He kicked with the other foot, and the cracks deepened. "Help me with this!" he said.

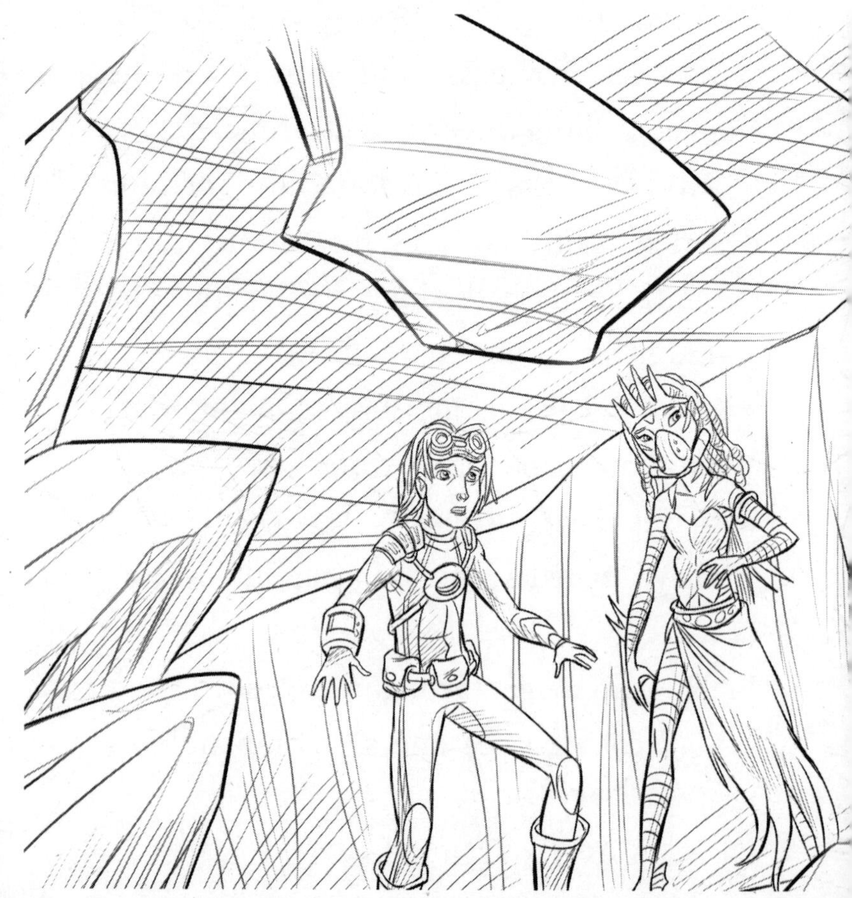

His mother charged the door with her shoulder, and the ice yielded, exploding inwards.

Wow! She's seriously strong! thought Max. If his mother had hurt herself, her calm face gave nothing away.

Max burst through, kicking the remaining shards loose. He found himself in a small chamber. "Jackpot!" he said. The room was filled with odd bits of tech and weaponry collected over the years. Max quickly selected an old-fashioned rocket launcher. Then he threw his mother a belt holding two blaster pistols. "Put that on!" he said.

Lia found an automated crossbow, loaded with deadly metal bolts.

"Let's go," she said grimly.

Max's mother fastened on the belt. "I certainly hope we defeat the fearsome monster," she said, her voice utterly toneless.

What's wrong with her? Max wondered. *It's like she's in some sort of trance.*

They'd taken just a few steps back into the passage when the other end collapsed completely in a shower of crumbling ice. A huge shifting shadow rose up behind the heaps of drifting debris.

As it cleared, and Max saw the terror causing the destruction, his feet wouldn't move.

"What on all Nemos is *that*?" he gasped.

CHAPTER EIGHT

BATTLING THE ROBOBEAST

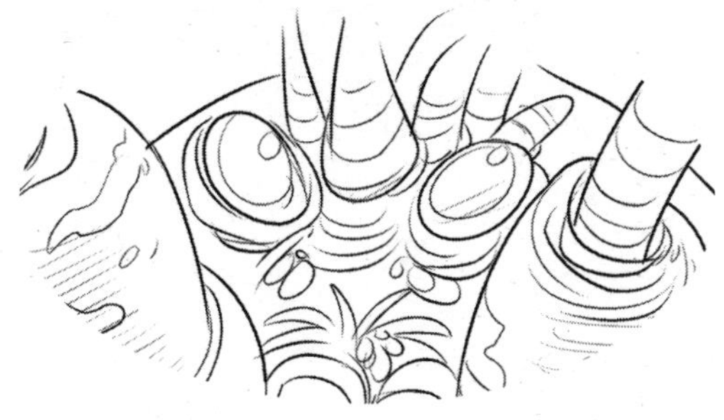

The creature looked like a lobster, but it was nothing like the ones the fishermen back on Aquora had caught in their pots. For one thing, it was at least a hundred times bigger than the biggest catch Max had ever seen, towering over him and his companions. Its blue shell looked thicker than a battleship's hull, and had been reinforced with shifting armour plating – titanium, Max guessed. Its claws, each bigger

than Max's aquabike, had been covered with metal cuffs. Glinting serrated edges tipped the pincers, making them sharper and more deadly still. A second set of claws extended from the creature's underbelly. As it lumbered through the passage, leaving a trail of destruction, Max spied a metal plaque on its shell. It said: *NEPHRO*.

"There's only one way out of here," said Max, nodding at the Beast. "Through that!"

He ran at the giant armoured lobster, which didn't seem to have noticed them and was busy smashing its mammoth pincers through any walls that remained standing. Max reached a broken section of floor and skidded to a halt. Looking down through the gap, he saw that much of the city mountain was in ruins already. Bridges had collapsed; whole sections of staircases were missing. The whole structure looked close to falling down.

We have to get out before this place becomes a tomb.

"Max, look down there!" Lia shouted,

pointing. "It's Spike!"

Max looked below and saw that a tank had been placed in the city's main square, several storeys beneath where they were standing. Flower garlands and wreaths hung from its sides.

Inside was Spike, swimming back and forth and obviously scared.

"We've got to rescue him," said Lia.

"We've got to stop Nephro," said Max's mum. "Get out of the way."

She drew one of the pistols from her waist and fired, dangerously close to Max's head. He watched as the blaster bolt smashed into Nephro's left claw. It bounced off harmlessly into a nearby wall, melting it to slush.

But it got Nephro's attention. The Robobeast twisted its body around to face them.

Max trembled to look into the swivelling

scarlet orbs of the lobster's eyes. On either side of its head, long antennae crackled with electricity, glowing blue.

He saw Lia touch her temples, eyes closed.

She's trying to communicate with her Merryn powers, he realised.

Nephro's mouthparts gaped and it gave a furious screech of anger.

"Not sure it wants to talk!" said Max. "Maybe it'll understand this."

Max fell to one knee, unclipped a rocket from the strap and dropped it into the magazine chamber. He lifted the rocket launcher onto his shoulder and took aim through the sights. As he pulled the trigger, the launcher jerked, almost throwing Max off balance. A rocket shot from the chamber, threading through the air on a trail of white smoke.

BOOM!

The rocket exploded into the side of Nephro's shell, rocking the Robobeast backwards.

When the smoke cleared, Max couldn't believe it. Apart from a black scorch mark, the rocket had had zero effect.

How can we possibly defeat this thing?

Nephro lunged towards them, all four claws darting and snapping. Max knew if he made just one wrong move he'd be cut in two. He dodged backwards, only to bump into his mother. She pushed him away from her, straight towards the serrated metal pincers.

"What are you doing?" Max yelled. He ducked as the claws sheared closed over his head. Another set came for him and he leaped over the top, landing on his front and sliding across the ice. The rocket launcher skittered out of his hands. He felt the creature's shadow fall over him and turned over. Nephro loomed above, its lower claws reaching to grab him.

"No!" Lia yelled. Max saw a crossbow bolt thud into a gap in Nephro's armour plating. The massive creature screeched and twisted away, writhing in pain. It rounded on Lia, antennae quivering. One of them arched towards her from above.

"Look out!" Max cried.

Too late. As Lia scrabbled backwards, the antenna lanced down and touched her shoulder, glowing an intense blue.

Her scream died in an instant and she went completely still.

Max clambered to his feet, staring in horror. Lia's features were white, her skin covered in a silvery frost. *She can't be…*

"She's frozen solid," said his mother, heading towards a descending staircase. As she disappeared, Nephro raised a giant claw above Lia's motionless body, ready to crush her into nothing.

CHAPTER NINE

TREACHERY

In a flash, Max had another rocket in the chamber and was pulling the trigger. The rocket slammed into the claw and knocked it off target. It crunched into the ice, just missing Lia. The creature backed away. *I hurt it*, Max thought, *but not enough.*

He dropped the weapon and dashed to Lia's side, rubbing her arms to try and warm her. They were rock hard and ice cold. Her eyes were still alive, and full of fear, but her limbs remained stiff.

As Nephro turned to face them again, Max hoisted his friend over his shoulder. "I'll get you out of here!" he said.

He began to hobble towards the staircase. The ice cracked and groaned with every step he took. Fragments broke free and tumbled downwards. He couldn't see his mother anywhere. *How could she leave me like that?* he wondered. Max chanced a look back. Nephro lingered above, antennae twitching, snapping at the air with its claws.

Max reached a gap where the ice had collapsed, and leaped over the abyss. Another two floors down, he reached the main square and Spike's tank, but he had no idea how he could free the swordfish while carrying his Merryn friend. The sound of thunder echoed from above, and Max glanced up. Nephro had stepped onto the ice stairs, and cracks were splintering through them. *It'll never*

hold, thought Max. Sure enough, the ice crumbled beneath the Robobeast's weight. In a shower of white, Max saw Nephro plunge downwards, claws waving desperately with nothing to grip. It landed with a thud in the main square, followed by tonnes of ice. The mountain shook as the blocks of ice crashed down, sending shockwaves across the ground. As the last of the debris shower hit the square, the air stilled. Nephro had vanished beneath the ice-fall.

"That's one less problem to worry about," Max muttered.

Now to release Spike.

HISSSS!

A blaster bolt singed the ice at his toes, stopping him in his tracks. He looked up from the steaming ground and saw the pistol in his mother's hand. She stood ten paces away.

"Where do you think you are going?" she said, her eyes cold.

"Mum?" said Max, his voice wavering. "Why… I don't understand…"

"Goodbye, Max," she said.

She raised the blaster and pointed it at his chest. Max sidestepped quickly, taking shelter behind Spike's tank. The swordfish swam back and forth, clearly alarmed to see Lia in danger.

"I want the key!" said his mother, pulling the trigger.

Her shot hit the tank, and glass exploded outwards. Warm water gushed over Max and Lia, sending him skidding off his feet. Spike flopped onto the ice, sliding and thrashing

in a shallow pool of water.

Lia moved at last, shivering as the warm water thawed her body.

Max saw his mother rushing at him, blaster raised.

This can't be happening!

He grabbed a chunk of ice and hurled it at her, sending the weapon spinning from her hand. She barrelled into him as he was standing, and they both fell onto the ice.

"Mum, stop!" he said.

"Give me the key!" she shouted, picking him up off the ground by his collar.

She hoisted him right off his feet and hurled him sideways. He slid across the ice, fetching up against a broken block. *How can she be so strong?*

"The key!" she said, striding towards him.

Max saw the mountain of ice debris behind her stir. An enormous blue claw broke through the surface.

Nephro…

His mother's hand closed over his throat and she lifted him off the ice. Max writhed, desperately trying to prise her fingers free.

"Give it to me, Max," she said.

He felt his breath failing. "Why are you doing this?" he croaked.

With her other hand, she reached inside his tunic.

Over his mother's shoulder, he saw the giant lobster shake the ice from its body and begin to drag itself towards them.

"Behind you!" Max tried to say, but the sound that came out was just a gurgle.

His mother pulled out the key, cackling horribly.

But just then Nephro's antennae lashed down on her back. Her fingers loosened their grip on Max's throat and he rolled clear. Lia helped him to his feet. Though her lips still looked blue, she seemed unhurt.

"My mum!" Max gasped.

His mother wasn't frozen like Lia had been. Her body juddered strangely, her fingers curling and uncurling. She barked odd, inhuman sounds over and over.

"What's wrong with her?" said Max.

Lia frowned. "She's speaking in different languages of the sea," she said. "She's saying 'I want the key'."

Nephro opened a pincer, reaching for his mother. Even though she'd just tried to kill him, Max's instincts took over. *I can't let my mother die!* He scanned the ground and saw her fallen pistol. He snatched it up and fired at the creature's head. The blast distracted it, but the laser bounced off, taking out another section of wall. Max fired again and again, driving Nephro away from his mother. Each time, the plating reflected the shot and another piece of the ice mountain dissolved.

"Max, stop!" said Lia. "You're destroying this place!"

Max aimed again. "I won't let it hurt my mother!" he shouted. He was about to pull the trigger again, when Lia grabbed his arm and tugged the pistol down.

"Enough!" she said. "Max, that thing, whatever it is, is not your mother."

Max stared into his friend's eyes. What was she saying? "But…" he began.

Nephro scooped up his mother in a pincer and lofted her high into the air with a screech of triumph. The Robobeast turned and lumbered towards a crumbled wall. Beyond, Max saw sky filled with snow flurries and open ocean. He realised there must be a long drop to the sea.

"No!" he yelled.

He shoved Lia out of his path and ran after Nephro, firing several shots. Some found their target, but others missed completely.

Through the gap, he saw the *Pride of Blackheart* lurking not far out to sea.

Nephro is going to take my mother to Cora and the Professor! I've got to stop them.

As Nephro reached the edge of the precipice Max took aim and fired again. The blast tipped the Robobeast off-balance, and its claws wheeled in the air, shaking Max's mother from side to side. Max leaped for her, throwing out his arms.

Then Nephro tumbled over the lip of ice, taking his mother with it.

CHAPTER TEN

HARD CHOICES

Max's fingers closed over his mother's arm.

His shoulder jarred, taking her weight as she dangled over the abyss. He caught the broken edge of the wall in his other hand, clinging on desperately. The Robobeast plummeted down the cliff towards the sea, rolling over and bouncing off the ice until it became tiny, then disappearing from view.

An icy wind whipped around him. Max gritted his teeth, and held on tightly to his mother's arm. *She's too heavy! I can't…*

His mother was still repeating "I want the key." She looked up, her eyes wide and staring, her mouth gaping.

Max almost screamed in horror. Inside his mother's throat he saw wires and metal. Circuits.

"No…" he mumbled. Was it the Professor's work? Her own brother? "Please, no. Not you too."

His mother's eyes focused on him. She smiled sweetly.

"Mum?" he said. "Is that you?"

She reached down with her free hand, unbuckled her second holster and drew out her remaining pistol.

"Mum, no!" Max shouted.

His mother brought the barrel round to point at his head, the same blank smile pasted on her face.

Max let go.

She fell without even a scream. Max rolled onto his back, unable to watch. He heard her body smashing off the cliff face below, and closed his eyes to stop the tears.

When he opened them again, Lia was standing over him. "I'm so sorry," she said. "It wasn't really her."

Max buried his face in his hands. "How do you know? It looked like her. What if the Professor implanted robotics in her, to make her evil?"

"What if he created that…thing from scratch?" said Lia. "He's done it with Robobeasts. Why not a robotic person?"

Max nodded, hoping in the depths of his heart that she was right. *If that thing wasn't my mum, perhaps she's still alive somewhere.*

"I found this," said Lia, holding up the key. "Your mother must have dropped it when Nephro zapped her."

Max took the key, gripping it tightly. Thank goodness Lia was still focusing on their mission. He slotted the key back into his pocket. *Time for me to forget my own troubles and focus along with her.*

"Let's go and check the Robobeast is

finished," he said.

Together, they picked their way down a narrow path in the mountainside. Out to sea, Cora's ship was retreating at full speed. *She knows she's failed again*, thought Max. He felt no triumph – Nephro's destruction was too great for that – only grim satisfaction.

As they neared the base of the slope, Max feared the worst. What if they found his mother's body, broken and cold? But when they reached the bottom there was no sign of her. Nephro lay on the icy shore, armour plating cracked and loose. The lobster's antennae drooped, and no blue energy crackled along their length. The creature reached out a claw weakly and let it flop. Pity surged through Max's chest.

"Is it dead?" Lia asked.

"I'm not sure," said Max. As he approached, the two red eyes swivelled towards him.

"It's all right," said Lia, her eyes closed. "It wants us to help free it."

Max edged forward, gripped one side of a piece of armour plating and heaved it loose. Lia joined him, and together they prised away the remains of the Professor's robotics. Beneath it, Nephro's body was unharmed.

The lobster's mouthparts opened and it gave several clicking sounds.

"You're welcome," said Lia.

Nephro clambered to its feet, shuffled towards the water, and slipped under the surface.

Another innocent creature set free, thought Max. *But at what cost?*

He and Lia climbed back towards the ruined city. As they worked their way up the path of ice, Max's communicator beeped. He pressed the earpiece and played the message from Rivet.

"Max! Found Max's dad! Gave warning! Aquora fleet ready! People thank Max! Dad thank Max! Stay safe!"

Thank goodness for that!

Max activated the microphone and hit transmit.

"Thanks, Riv, remain on standby. I'll be in

touch soon with our next destination."

They reached the hole broken in the mountainside and entered the Arctirian city. The tall blue inhabitants were slowly emerging from hiding, wailing at the destruction.

"It'll take years to rebuild!" one cried. "Our beautiful, beautiful homes are gone!"

"Perhaps you should have fought for them," Lia muttered under her breath, so only Max could hear.

They found Spike being tended to by several Arctirians. They were pouring more warm water into his shallow pool. One of them was the female leader.

"Thank you for looking after our friend," said Lia.

The blue woman smiled, for the first time since Max had met her. "But he's so beautiful," she said. "Why does he hang around with two repulsive creatures like you?"

"I'm not sure whether to take that as a compliment or not," said Lia.

"Think nothing of it," said a human voice. Max saw Jonah walking towards them, grinning. "They don't mean to be rude. It's just their way." His face became serious. "You still have the key?"

Max tapped his pocket. "Thanks to Lia."

Jonah nodded. "Then you must go to the city of Gustados next," he said. "That's where the third key can be found. Cora will be heading there next, since it's not as well defended as Aquora."

Gustados – the third city in the Alliance. Another Quest. Another Robobeast of the Professor's making.

Max pushed his weariness away. "Will you come with us?" he asked. "We could use someone who knows Cora well."

Jonah shook his head. "My place is here," he

said, "but listen..." He gripped Max's arm. "Be careful. Cora is ruthless. She'll do anything to get the keys, and she'll never give up."

"Don't worry," said Max. "Neither will we."

Max didn't know what lay ahead of them. He didn't know what other deadly Robobeasts the Professor had created, or if he'd ever meet his real mother. He just knew one thing – they would keep fighting, no matter what.

"Ready, Max?" asked Lia. He turned to her and saw her eyes shining with determination.

Max nodded.

"Ready," he said.

Don't miss Max's next Sea Quest adventure, when he faces

FINARIA
THE SAVAGE SEA SNAKE

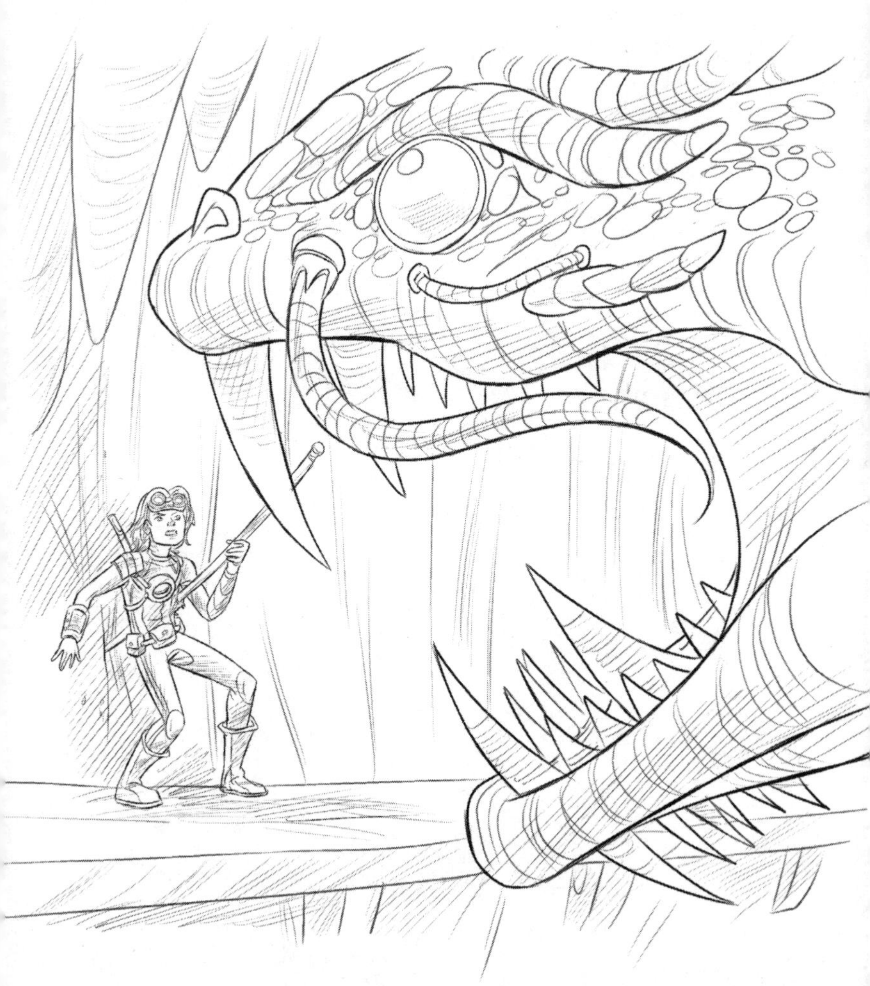

SEA
QUEST ®

Look out for all the books in

Sea Quest Series 4:

THE LOST LAGOON

REKKAR THE SCREECHING ORCA

TRAGG THE ICE BEAR

HORVOS THE HORROR BIRD

GUBBIX THE POISON FISH

OUT IN SEPTEMBER 2014!

Don't miss the

BRAND NEW

Special Bumper Edition:

SKALDA

THE SOUL STEALER

978 1 40832 851 4

OUT IN JUNE 2014

WIN AN EXCLUSIVE GOODY BAG

In every Sea Quest book the Sea Quest logo is hidden in one of the pictures. Find the logos in books 9-12, make a note of which pages they appear on and go online to enter the competition at

www.seaquestbooks.co.uk

Each month we will put all of the correct entries into a draw and select one winner to receive a special Sea Quest goody bag.

You can also send your entry on a postcard to:

Sea Quest Competition, Orchard Books,
338 Euston Road, London, NW1 3BH

Don't forget to include your name and address!

GOOD LUCK

Closing Date: May 31st 2014

Competition open to UK and Republic of Ireland residents. No purchase required.
For full terms and conditions please see www.seaquestbooks.co.uk

DARE YOU DIVE IN?

www.seaquestbooks.co.uk

Deep in the water lurks a new breed of Beast.

Dive into the new Sea Quest website to play games, download activities and wallpapers and read all about Robobeasts, Max, Lia, the Professor and much, much more.

Sign up to the newsletter at www.seaquestbooks.co.uk to receive exclusive extra content, members-only competitions and the most up-to-date information about Sea Quest.

DON'T MISS THE

BRAND NEW SERIES OF:

Series 14: THE CURSED DRAGON

978 1 40832 920 7

978 1 40832 921 4

978 1 40832 922 1

978 1 40832 923 8

OUT NOW!